# Especially for you . . .

This is the season for sharing, and we'd like to share with you, our Harlequin friends, this special Christmas story.

Written by popular North American romance author Lucy Agnes Hancock, *Christmas Gift* touches on the importance of family ties, the unexpected blossoming of a new love and the tender rediscovery of an old.

We hope you'll treasure this unique and moving story. It is sent with our deepest appreciation and best wishes for the coming year.

Sincerely,
Harlequin Reader Service
Christmas, 1981

# Christmas Gift

Lucy Agnes Hancock

## *Harlequin Books*

TORONTO • LONDON • LOS ANGELES • AMSTERDAM
SYDNEY • HAMBURG • PARIS • STOCKHOLM • ATHENS • TOKYO

Harlequin edition published December 1960

Second printing December 1981

ISBN 0-373-00562-8

Printed in Canada

*To you fortunate ones who still believe in the old customs, old traditions and whose hearts and footsteps turn homeward at Christmastime*

# Chapter One

*A Christmas Wish*

JOAN MARSH awakened to the blare of an automobile horn below her window. She sat up, shivered and hastily pulled the blankets about her shoulders. The clock on the stand suddenly shamed her into springing out of bed. Nine o'clock! She slipped her feet into furry mules, caught up a robe and ran to the open window.

"Go away!" she ordered the blond young man in the noisy roadster. "Can't a woman be allowed to have even a few hours' sleep?"

"You're just plain lazy, Joan." The young man grinned up at her. "Come on over to the farm with me. It's a swell day for skiing. Come on, we'll have a lot of fun."

"No can do, Charles." Joan was not too regretful. "I have a date at the Neighborhood House at ten-thirty and shall be busy until after four. Life is real, life is earnest, Charles, and mere fun is not its goal, or words to that effect. Run along, my good man—maybe Mitzy Bush will go with you."

"How long is this slumming going to last?" Charles asked, aggrieved.

"Until after the Christmas party, and it's not slumming. Those youngsters are darling, even if their names aren't in the social register. Go 'long and find yourself another playmate."

"Aw, Joan, honey, don't be like that!"

But with a determined and final "Bye, Charles!" Joan slammed down the window. She stood listening for a moment and smiled wistfully when the car roared down the drive.

*Why couldn't it have been Tom out there,* she mused. *But no; right now Tom is probably standing before a roomful of students explaining the theory of soil conservation—or something.* The gray eyes softened and the smile became tender. *Dear, proud, sensitive, stubborn darling! Will you ever realize that love isn't measured in dollars and cents?*

The telephone rang and she lifted the receiver of the extension. "Is that you, Joan? When do you expect to be here? We're all waiting."

"Be with you in twenty minutes, Alice. Hold everything. But sa-ay, what's the rush? Mrs. Foster said ten-thirty. Oh, all right—twenty minutes or so. Bye!"

Ten minutes later she was standing in the breakfast room, a coffee cup in one hand while the other shuffled the pile of mail at her father's place.

"Your father left early," Aunt Fanny offered. "Some important man had to see him on business. He has to be back by nine or nine-thirty. Beulah's cross. You know how she hates a late breakfast. What's the matter with you?"

Joan had picked a thick square gray envelope from the pile and was holding it gingerly by one corner, her pretty nose wrinkling in distaste. "Irma Bessemer! Why is she writing to Dad?"

"I'm sure I don't know." Aunt Fanny's tone was virtuously and deceptively noninquisitive. "And you must eat something if you are going down to that smelly Neighborhood House."

"I think you do know, Aunt Fan, and the Neighborhood House is not smelly." She slid the thick gray envelope to the bottom of the pile, pocketed the three letters belonging to her, swallowed the last of her coffee, caught up her fur coat and left the

12

room. Two minutes later she was racing down the drive.

It was after six when she returned, and Aunt Fanny was displeased, for Charles Austin had telephoned twice. She considered Joan very much of a fool to risk losing the most eligible bachelor in the community.

"Don't say it, Aunt Fan," Joan advised as she prepared to mount the stairs. "I simply couldn't get away earlier. I practically had to carve every single note of 'Holy Night' into the brains of those kids. It's work, I'm telling you."

"Why, I supposed every child in the world knew 'Holy Night'—"

"So did I, until today. These poor little waifs are newcomers. Their dads work on that new dam, and the Neighborhood House gathered in the children. Mrs. Foster turned them over to me. You see, my dear aunt, I'm supposed to possess patience and finesse—attributes so essential to a good teacher." Aunt Fanny gave a refined sniff. "Of course," Joan explained, "two of the nine are mere babies, but the others range from six to ten. I imagine next time it won't be so hard—they must have absorbed something. I'll be down in time for dinner all right. Is Dad home?"

"Not yet, but probably he will be very soon. Charles will be here for dinner, Joan. Now, now—" as the girl made a grimace "—the boy practically invited himself. What could I do?"

"Oh, I believe you—with reservations—Aunt Fan," Joan muttered as she went on up the stairs. "Charles fancies he's welcome anywhere, anytime. If he only knew! And I wanted to be sure Dad is going to keep his promise for the holidays."

It wasn't until dinner was over, and Charles, after vainly urging Joan to go over to Berwicks to dance, had rather huffily departed, that the girl found the opportunity for a brief talk with her father.

"How about it, Dad? Is everything all

right? We're surely going to Gran's for Christmas?"

David Marsh dropped his paper and looked at his daughter, tall, slim and very lovely in her pale yellow dinner dress. Now why on earth should a popular young girl like Joan want to go off to the country for the holidays? And to such a quiet, dead-alive country as that around the Marsh homestead back in New York State.

Why, the nearest village was four miles away, and Corinth all of twenty. No—he shook his head—it wouldn't do at all. Aunt Fanny was right: it was much better to accept Mrs. Bessemer's invitation for her Christmas Eve party. In fact, the lady had hinted that the party was really for Joan—and her late husband's wealthy young cousin, Charles Austin. Charles Austin appeared decidedly interested in Joan.

David Marsh frowned, then sighed. He supposed it was bound to come sooner or later, and as Aunt Fanny and Mrs. Bessemer had tactfully pointed out to him, young Austin was the direct answer to a doting parent's prayer. Still, Joan was young; surely there was plenty of time, and yet....

"No, my dear," he said decidedly. "Not for the Christmas holidays. You have no idea how dull it is there in the winter. Nothing going on—no young people— why, you'd be bored to death. And then, too, Father and Mother are getting old, you know. Excitement isn't too good for them. None of the others are going home— not even Ann, who is nearest.

"I'm sure they feel, as I do, that at their age Christmas can't mean a great deal, and to have a houseful of people descend on them, entailing extra work—cooking, cleaning and so on.... No, Joan, it just wouldn't do."

"But...but, Dad. They want—they expect—" Joan began.

"You were there in the summer," her father reminded her.

"Yes, and I loved it. Gran's a darling and Gramp's an old peach!"

"That's just it, my dear. One visit a year is quite sufficient. And it's much better that the visits be by just one or two at a time and of not too long duration. You see, Joan, while Mother and Father are apparently well, they are both in their seventies."

"Oh, Dad!" Joan exclaimed. "What if they are? I'm sure they would love having us—all of us."

"Absolutely not, my dear. They invite us, of course; but I'm sure—we're all sure—they must be relieved that none of us accept. And you must remember, Joan, we are all busy people."

Joan took her hand from the mantel where she was standing and clasped it tightly behind her back. Her gray eyes sparkled dangerously and her voice was scornful.

"Busy! I . . . I think you're a lot of smug, selfish—"

"Now, now, my dear," her father soothed. "We are not selfish. I've had letters from all my brothers and sisters and every one of us sent a generous check. I mailed mine this morning. We feel sure that the money will do them far more good than a brief, exciting visit, and it isn't as if we didn't see them during the year. With the exception of Henry in France, we've all visited them within the year. No, Joan, I'm sure there is not a family living that is more affectionate, generous and thoughtful than the Marsh family!"

"Affectionate! Generous! Thoughtful! Dad, how can you?"

"Did you send off your gifts as I advised, my dear?" Mr. Marsh ignored his daughter's indignant outburst.

"Yes, I did."

"Then, that's all right. You see? They will not be expecting us and so won't be disappointed."

"I sent them ahead because you said we would go by plane, Dad," Joan reminded him.

"I said, *if* we go, my dear," her father amended a bit impatiently. "Now run along, child. I've had a hard day and wish to be quiet." Joan turned to leave the room. He spoke again. "Oh, by the way, my dear, Mrs. Bessemer is giving a large party on the twenty-fourth. She thinks we, er, you will find it amusing."

But if Joan heard, she made no comment, and the door closed before he had quite finished his remark. David Marsh sighed. No doubt it was as Aunt Fanny and Mrs. Bessemer had pointed out to him. Joan was too much alone. She needed a younger woman in the house with her. If only Ellen could have lived! But there was no use wishing for the impossible. He had never seriously considered remarrying. However, Irma Bessemer was a most attractive woman. . . .

AT HER DESK in her charming sitting room upstairs, Joan was writing letters. She wrote steadily for hours and sometimes she grinned wickedly, sometimes she frowned, and sometimes her eyes filled with bright tears, which she succeeded in winking back. She sealed and stamped the last letter just as she heard her father come upstairs. He paused at her door and knocked softly.

Joan sat very still for a moment, and he walked on. Contritely, she flew to the door and called, "Did you want me, Dad?"

"No. Oh, no. Just wanted to say goodnight, my dear."

Joan kissed him. "Good night, Daddy. Sleep well!"

# Chapter Two

❄

*Holiday Memories*

IN THE OLD MARSH HOMESTEAD back in
New York State, a bit later in the week,
Mrs. Marsh folded her third letter and
sighed softly as she laid it on top of the
others.

"Dave not coming, either?" questioned
her husband, hearing the sigh.

"Not coming either, Father. A Mrs. Bessemer's giving a dinner dance for Joan on Christmas Eve. Dave hints that maybe Joan is going to marry that young Austin after all, and I'm sorry, Father, though maybe I shouldn't be. But it seems to me Joan's too fine for an idler like Charley Austin, even if he is worth a mint of money. I'm sure it's her Aunt Fanny that's engineered the whole affair, Father. David doesn't seem to take much interest in things outside his business. Maybe if Ellen had lived.... Well, Father, it looks like we spend Christmas alone—again."

"Don't you care, Lady," Mr. Marsh responded, trying to show an indifference he was far from feeling. "It'll be just like when we were first married. 'Member that first Christmas, Mother, an' how we had a cute little tree an' hung a catnip ball onto it for the cat an' a box of some newfangled dog biscuits for old...Rex, 'twas, wasn't it? 'Member how we drove over to Wellsburg to church an' what a lovely mornin' it was? Seems like I'll never forget that first

Christmas in our own home, Lady—just the two of us.''

"It wasn't just two of us long, though, was it, Father?" the old lady mused. "The second Christmas we had Martha. Do you remember how we hung up her stocking between ours? Wasn't she the cutest thing you ever saw? Seemed to know even then what it was all about. Then pretty soon there were five little stockings between yours and mine, and every year they grew longer and longer, and then first thing we knew, one after another they just disappeared. One after another the children went away to homes of their own, and—never again found it possible, somehow, all to be here at the same time. It's four years since our stockings have had company, Father.

"But...I'm not grieving, dear. It's right, I suppose, that they should live their own lives in their own way—only, at Christmas I miss them so, Father, don't you?"

"Miss 'em? Sure, I miss 'em," Mr.

Marsh assured her heartily, "but that fact
ain't goin' to spoil my day for me. Not a
bit of it. We'll have a tree for the cat an'
dog. Young Romeo an' old Juliet'll get a
big kick out of it, I'll warrant. An',
Mother, weather permittin', we'll drive
over to Wellsburg on Christmas mornin'
like we did nearly fifty years ago, an'—
Why, Lady, it'll be like old times!
Or... listen, Mother, what say we invite
Janet Frost for the holidays? I just bet
she'd love it."

"Let's do, Father, and maybe young
Tom Hallock would like to come out
again. He's never been here in winter. How
crazy he was about the farm last summer,
and what a time Joan and he had! Seems
like Joan's the only one who likes the
farm, but I expect young Austin has cured
her of that by this time. For a while there, I
thought she and Tom.... D'you know,
Father, I was kind of sorry you didn't let
him have a try at working that South
Farm. After all, if a body loves his work,
he's bound to get on."

"Theoretic farmers may be all right, Mother," offered Mr. Marsh, glad to get the subject away from the absent children, "but I'm old-fashioned, an' maybe set in my ways; an' you see, Mother, he wasn't married nor had no prospec's, so he said; an' you know, that South Farm's got to have a woman onto it. I sort of fancied there one spell that he liked our Joan, but I s'pose she'd never be willin' to settle down onto a farm—her Aunt Fanny'd see to that. Tom's a likely youngster, though, an' they think a lot of him down at the agricultural college, I'm told. You wait a minute, Mother. I'll get 'em both on the telephone an' find out if they can come."

Both could and would, and with Christmas only a week off, Mr. Marsh felt satisfied that his wife would find little time for brooding over the absence of the family.

Janet Frost arrived after school closed on Thursday night, and young Hallock on Friday morning. Janet was like a daughter of the house. In fact, she was just David

Marsh's age—forty-five—and had gone to school with the Marsh children.

There had been a time when Mrs. Marsh had hoped that she and David would make a match of it, but David fell in love with beautiful Ellen Carter during his senior year in college, married her almost at once and went to Michigan to work for Ellen's father, manufacturing woodenware.

If Janet was hurt, she never showed it. Her smile flashed as hearteningly and her voice rang as cheerily as ever. With the passing of her parents, her visits to the Marsh home became more frequent, and even now that she was teaching at the Annesley high school, nearly a hundred miles away, she managed to run in quite often. She and Helga, the hired girl, were busy in the kitchen when Tom Hallock arrived.

"It's mighty nice of you to have me out here, Mrs. Marsh," the young man said as he shook hands with his hostess. "I haven't spent a Christmas in the country since I was a youngster. Tell me, what do I

28

smell? Fruit cake? Mince pies? Ginger-
bread?''

''Fruit cake? Fie, Tom!'' smiled Mrs.
Marsh. ''The fruit cakes and plum pud-
dings were made a month ago. That's spice
cookies you smell. Janet's making them. I
taught her when she was about eight.
Jan-et!'' she called. ''Come here and meet
Tom Hallock.''

Tom was relieved when he saw that his
fellow guest was middle-aged. He had been
a little afraid that these dear old people
were attempting a bit of matchmaking,
and, well, he couldn't stand that. He hoped
he hadn't shown his dismay when Mr.
Marsh had tactfully broken the news of
Joan's pending engagement. Joan hadn't
said anything about it in her last letter to
him, received a month ago. She had joked
a little about how Charley Austin was giving her a grand rush, showing off his cars,
his horses and his mansions.

Simply rolling in money, Tom, and I
can't for the life of me see any reason

for his sudden infatuation. I know I'm sort of nice, Tom, because you told me so once, when you were feeling 'specially sentimental— 'member? Sometimes I think you're abnormally dumb, Tommy....

Charley's one attraction for me is his country estate. It's marvelous! It's colossal! It's stupendous! Simply acres and acres, Tom, with the swankiest private golf course and a pool that would put your eye out. He calls it The Farm, but I've never seen a chicken, nor a pig, nor even a cow, during my visits there, and if they grow the plebian onion or the lowly cabbage on the place, they keep it dark. Farm? It is to laugh, my friend! We know what a farm should be, don't we?

He had answered that letter two weeks later and had tried to keep the love and longing for her out of his reply. What had he to offer a girl like Joan? To be sure, this year would find him out of debt and his own man again, but it would be years before he would be making more than a living. His salary was twenty-one hundred a year, and after this year he couldn't be sure of even that amount, for he was determined to give up teaching and tackle farming. Well, they travel fastest who travel alone, and it looked like a lonely journey for Tom Hallock, for he was certain that no other girl had the power to erase from his heart and life the indelible impression made by Joan Marsh.

One thing was certain, however: these two dear old people must never know. Joan, their only grandchild, was the apple of their eye and they were already unhappy at the thought of her marriage to this Austin fellow. No need to add to it. From what Mr. Marsh had said on their drive down from the station, Mrs. Marsh was grieving that none of the sons and daughters had found it possible to tear themselves away from their social or business interests even for a day or two.

They had, somehow, banked on Joan's being different. She, of them all, had loved the old place, and now she, too, was about to go over to the Egyptians.

"It's been in the family more than a hundred years, this farm has, Tom," Mr. Marsh pointed out as they began the slow ascent from the village. "But I s'pose when Mother an' I pass on it will be sold to strangers. Maybe Dave'll keep the wood lot an' the old grove yonder, to turn into wooden bowls an' bobbins. None of 'em can find anything to love in the land, it seems, though." He sighed regretfully. "Henry's turned into a Frenchman—ain't been back here in six years. Hugh finds northern winters too severe for him! Umph! Goes to Florida every November an' stays 'til May. A darn' smart lawyer, Hugh is, an' he's made a pile of money. Guess it's his wife and golf take him south each year, an' not a weak constitution. Of course, Martha's kept busy helpin' her delicate husband run a fruit ranch out in California. I guess that lets her out, an'

Ann, our youngest, is livin' in one of these here penthouses in New York an' tryin' to make an artist out of a mighty fine sign painter. Maybe you've heard of Ann's husband—Nickolas Barnard, his name is. You have heard of him? I thought so. Lots of publicity about his stuff.

"Well, Tom, there's the family roster. Guess maybe I wa'n't much good as a father. What say?"

"Why, Mr. Marsh, your sons and daughters are all successful and two of them are quite famous. You shouldn't feel that you have failed just because none of your children have the farming instinct," soothed Tom.

"Who's talkin' about farmin' instinct, Tom?" the old man demanded. "It's love for their mother I'm talkin' about. Those youngsters had the best mother God ever put on this earth, an' how do they treat her?

"Say, listen. We got five checks for Christmas presents from our children! Fine, eh? Money, money—that's all they ever send. Easiest way out—no time to spend in searchin' for a gift for the one who spent weeks an' months workin' on little s'prises for them, 'way back when money wa'n't any too plentiful.

"I'll say for Joan, though, that she's been some different. She sent a box covered with Santa Claus and Don't-Open-Until-Christmas stickers—grand! Just tickled us to see the way 'twas done up. Joan's always sendin' s'prises to her grandmother an' me. You know, Tom, I don't give a snap of my finger for myself. It's for Mother my blood boils! For Lady, bless her sweet heart!"

"I'm sure they are just thoughtless, sir. Too much prosperity is apt to make one like that, I'm afraid," murmured Tom, distressed for the old man.

"Maybe so, Tom. Maybe so. But I kind of wish Joan wasn't goin' to marry this Austin chap. I been hopin' that she'd take over the farm someday, but I guess this sort of puts the kibosh onto that hope, don't it?"

Tom was glad they were nearing the house and he wasn't called upon to reply.

# Chapter
# Three

❄

*Unexpected Arrivals*

As he unpacked his bag in the big sunny
bedroom assigned him, Tom Hallock
determined to prove a cheering guest to
these kindly hosts; that is, if a light heart, a
healthy appetite and a fund of nonsense
would suffice. How could children be so
cruel, so forgetful? Life was pitiless to the
aged. If his parents had been spared, Tom
told himself, nothing under heaven could
have kept him from being with them on

these special occasions. But that was it. Those who had such a bounty of treasure so seldom appreciated it. Life was queer that way.

There was no sign of heartache during the delightful midday meal, however, and Tom and his host were like two small boys, full of spirits and occasionally even a little naughty. They all loved it and very soon found that they were exerting no effort to appear happy—they just were happy.

Tom and Janet hung wreaths in the windows, then strung lights through the spruce boughs that filled the long porch boxes and in among the branches of the small firs that flanked the steps.

Afterward the quartet drove over to the county seat for last-minute shopping, meeting every few minutes to compare notes and offer advice. They came home to a house glowing warmly in the gathering darkness, the wreath-hung windows ablaze with light.

*Helga remembered,* Janet and Tom both thought, and marveled. Helga had appeared so unsympathetic to their plans—so stolid, so dumb. The old folks felt a glow of pleasure that their guests had planned this spectacle for them.

"Pretty, eh, Tom?" beamed Mr. Marsh as Tom drove the car in through the gate and slowly circled the front of the house.

"Beautiful, sir!" An unaccountable lump in his throat prevented him from saying more. These splendid old people, carrying on in spite of their lonely hearts! Carrying on with bands playing—banners waving! It was grand!

They let Janet and Mrs. Marsh out at the front door and then drove to the barn.

"Now say, Tom, you leave my stuff right here. I'll tie 'em up after supper an' sneak 'em in the back way. An 'say, Tom, are you sure Janet'll like that fancy wrapper an' them floppy slippers with bunches of feathers onto 'em? They look kind of queer to me." Mr. Marsh was a bit doubtful of Tom's taste when it came to women's apparel.

"Sure. She'll love them. Dean Elkins

bought his wife a negligee and matching mules almost like yours for her birthday, and he said she was crazy about them. Miss Frost reminds me of Mrs. Elkins—friendly and yet dignified. I hope she won't think I'm fresh because I added a scarf to the box of candy I bought her. It seems as if I've always known her.''

"Oh, Janet's like that," his host assured him. "Friendly as a kitten and 'll be pleased as Punch that a good-lookin' young feller like you'd choose a swell scarf for a woman old enough to be his mother. D'you know, Tom, when I look at Janet Frost, I'm always thoroughly convinced in my own mind that as a sex, men are dumb—yes, sir, dumb. Janet's one of the Lord's own anointed. I know of only one woman any sweeter, an' that's Lady.

"An' yet she's been allowed to remain single. Oh, she's had chances—good men, too; but they all lacked stick-to-itiveness. That's what got me Lady, son. That an' a consumin' love that drove me on to pass all the also-ran's an' kept me follerin' till I guess she felt so sorry for me, hangin' 'round, she had to say yes to get any peace. D'you know, Tom, love's a wonderful thing! It's powerful, too.. Seems though it can perform miracles. Nothin' like it in this whole wide world. I wish I could be sure in my own mind that Joan really loves this Austin chap, but— Yes, Mother. We're coming,'' as a long halloo came from the house.

"D'you know this Charley feller, Tom?'' queried the old man anxiously as they put out the lights and shut the barn doors.

"No, sir, I've never met him. But I think you may rest assured that Joan will never marry a man she doesn't love. If she marries this Charles Austin, why, it is conclusive evidence that she must love him, it seems to me, Mr. Marsh.''

Tom spoke grimly. He didn't want to talk about Joan—even to think about her. Time enough for that when he was back in his lonely room and in the stark years ahead.

"Maybe you're right, Tom. Maybe—but, oh, pshaw! Now, all together:

"Jingle bells, jingle bells,
  Jingle all the way;
  Oh, what fun it is to ride
  In a one-horse open sleigh."

Singing lustily and prancing like a pair of skittish colts, the two entered the warm kitchen.

"You boys better behave yourselves—supper's getting cold and Helga's fit to be tied." Mrs. Marsh appeared strangely excited as she bustled about between kitchen and dining room. Where was Janet Frost, Tom wondered. "I wouldn't blame her a mite, Father, if she refused to keep your victuals hot sometimes—you dawdle so."

"Not Helga; she's too fond of me. Ain't you, Helga?" teased the old man, smiling at the hired girl, whose stolid face was split in a wide and wholly unaccustomed grin.

"*Ja*," she retorted, and still grinning broadly, she went into the pantry.

There was a smothered laugh, and two slim hands covered Mr. Marsh's eyes for a moment.

"Ann—Annie, girl!" her father cried, catching her in his arms. "Wh-where did you come from?"

"The big wicked city, Daddy, where they don't know how to keep Christmas. Oh, but it's grand to be home again!"

"Did Nickolas come—" Mr. Marsh began.

"Mm-mm." She shook her satiny dark head. "Nick's gone to an important client's over the holidays, so I ran away. Glad to see me, darlings? Oh, and you are Tom Hallock, Dad's white-haired boy—I was going to say 'foster son.' I know. He simply raved about you when I was here in the fall."

Ann Barnard talked fast. She was a little like Joan, Tom thought, only more sophisticated—more brittle.

Janet came in and they sat down to supper.

"Helga's young man is coming for her at

43

half-past seven. They're going to a dance, Father Marsh," explained Janet as Helga retired to the kitchen.

"Dance?" marveled Tom, recalling the awkward bulk of the Swedish girl. "Gee, I'd give a dollar to see her."

"Oh, they're not bad at all," said Janet who had attended dances in Little Sweden, "nor ungraceful, either. Certainly they are dignified and somehow a relief from the ugly posturing and fantastic gyrations that go by the name of dancing nowadays. I'm sorry, Ann. You see, I'm very much of a schoolmarm and have no doubt grown a bit prudish."

"You prudish, Jan!" laughed Ann. "A bit awe-inspiring, perhaps, but never prudish—you couldn't be." There was real affection in her voice.

"You an' Dave sure set the pace twenty-five, thirty years ago, Janet. A purtier pair I never hope to see," recalled Mr. Marsh.

"Anyone would dance well with David as partner, Father Marsh," laughed

Janet, entirely without self-consciousness. "I'm not doing much dancing now."

They talked of old times, when the Marsh children had gone to the little red brick schoolhouse, long since demolished.

"These here new consolidated schools, Janet," Mr. Marsh asked. "D'you honestly consider them as good as the old one-roomer?"

"From the viewpoint of progress and educational advantages, yes, absolutely, Father Marsh," Janet replied.

"Pshaw!" the old man sputtered. "That ain't what I meant a-tall. An' anyway, I have my doubts if these here newfangled schools'll turn out any better men an' women than the little red one-roomers."

Tom Hallock laughed. "There were giants in those days, Mr. Marsh."

"You're right, Tom. Grand big folks— both as teachers an' scholars, too. An' what times we used to have! Them were the days, Tom! Eh, Lady?"

"But the world moves on, Father," Mrs. Marsh said softly.

"And you wouldn't want to go back to them," Ann contributed. "No cars, no tractors, no radio, no telephone—"

"But all five of our children," her father reminded her. "All five of 'em."

"You run along and dress, Helga," Mrs. Marsh said tactfully as dessert was brought in. "We'll do up the supper dishes. Better take a blanket along and roll up warm coming back. It's going to be a cold night. And, Helga, stop at the upper farm and leave the papers and that basket of things I brought from town, will you, please? I want Mrs. O'Hara to have it for the tree. Have a nice time, Helga."

"*Ja*. Thanks, Mis' Marsh," and Helga departed with no change of gait.

"Such spirits! Such enthusiasm! Don't it wonder you?" grinned Mr. Marsh, back in his role of clown.

"Helga's got a poker face, sir. Probably she's thrilled and excited and has a blood pressure of two hundred and forty at this very minute," laughed Tom.

"Not our Helga. First of all, she's got

ice water in her veins, an' in the second place, she ain't got a heart, so how can she feel either great joy or deep sorrow?'' Mr. Marsh explained.

"Lucky Helga!" murmured Tom, and blushed to his ears in embarrassment at the sudden silence.

The old people exchanged glances and Janet's eyes grew tender with understanding. Only Ann was puzzled. Mrs. Marsh rose briskly.

"Suppose you boys put up the tree in the parlor and get down the trimmings from the attic. You'll find them all in boxes and labeled. And don't drop a thing. The girls and I will do up the dishes. 'Twon't take long. Don't you two get to cutting up any capers, either," she admonished. "Hurry right along—we've got a lot to do."

"Yes, ma'am," came in submissive falsetto as Tom and his host hurried away.

"Dear me, Janet, I just feel in my bones that Tom Hallock is more than half in love with Joan. That poor boy!"

"With our Joan, Mother!" Ann was

47

aghast. This poor young teacher! It was, of course, a pity, but how preposterous! Bright, sparkling, beautiful Joan Marsh was destined for something better than being the wife of a small-college professor.

"I sort of suspicioned it last summer and half expected him to propose," her mother went on, blind to the disapproval in Ann's face. "But maybe he thought he wasn't in a position to marry, and then, too, Joan's Aunt Fanny's all for this Austin man. Why, land only knows. It can't be just his money, though he's very rich, I understand. But Joan will have plenty. She needn't marry any man just because he's wealthy. Maybe it's social position. Maybe Charley Austin is 'way up in society. I wouldn't know about that. But—"

"Charley Austin!" cried Ann. "Charley Austin! Why, Mother, Charley Austin is—"

"Now, don't tell me he's a fine match, Ann," the old lady protested. "He's got a lot of money and does nothing but gad about all over creation doing a lot of perfectly useless things. I want Joan should have a better, finer life than gallivanting around the world with him."

Ann Barnard shook her head in good-natured helplessness. "Oh, Mother! You are incurably romantic!"

"And thank goodness for that!" Mrs. Marsh retorted vigorously.

"Oh, but, Mother Marsh, maybe Joan really loves this Austin man. I don't think David would ever consent to her marrying him if she didn't, do you?" asked Janet thoughtfully as she rinsed the tumblers.

"David? Umph! I could shake that boy, Janet. Woodenware! Wooden bowls, wooden rolling pins, five-percent reduction in woodenware manufacturing cost! That's all David thinks about, Janet. I thought when Ellen died he'd wake up, but he didn't. Guess he's become wooden himself from working in it so much. Joan seems to think he adores her, but I don't know. She thinks the world of him, that's certain. I wish he'd marry again, Janet. Fanny

Carter doesn't make a home for him nor for Joan, either."

"But who would want a wooden man, Mother Marsh?" laughed Janet. "There, that's all. Where are those boys? I'll warrant they are up to mischief. Do you know, Mother Marsh, I'm having the best time! And what a fine fellow Tom Hallock is! How could any girl with a chance at him let him get away? If only I were twenty years younger!"

"You were never more attractive than you are right now, my dear," Mrs. Marsh declared.

"Mother's right, Jan," Ann agreed, an arm around the waist of each. "You add new beauty with every year—a very special kind of beauty. I'll have to study your methods, my dear."

There came a long, insistent summons from the doorbell, and Ann ran down the hall to answer it.

"Merry Christmas! Merry Christmas!"

A slim dark man and a short, decidedly plump woman in a raccoon coat much too large for her stamped the snow from their feet and stepped inside. Janet Frost held Mrs. Marsh close for a moment, then released her to the embrace of Martha Endicott and Hugh Marsh. There was the sound of running feet, and Mr. Marsh came hurrying down the stairs followed by Tom Hallock, who was literally up to his eyes in tree decorations.

"Well, if this ain't a grand s'prise, I'll eat my Sunday shirt!" As he hugged them both, their father sputtered questions. "Wh-where? Wh-what—"

"By plane, Father," explained Martha breathlessly. "Hugh from Florida and I from California, and the queer thing is, we met in the Corinth airport."

"Yes," drawled Hugh, his gray eyes twinkling. "I saw what appeared to be six coon-skinned coeds trying to convince a bewildered taxi driver there was only one fare under that expanse of fur and giving him vague directions. Fortunately I caught the name Wellsburg and examined the animated bale of hides more closely, only to find it enclosed my own sister!"

There was a general laugh, and Mrs. Marsh patted Martha's sleeve.

"And John, dear?"

"Oh, John's having a friend of his down from San Francisco. A fraternity brother and an old bachelor. They'll have a grand time."

"Where in the world did you unearth that coat, Mat?" Ann asked in disgust. "It can't possibly be yours—I hope."

"Of course not, silly. I have no need of a fur coat. Mrs. Wilson, a friend of mine, insisted on my wearing it. She was lovely about it."

"Lovely!" scoffed Ann. "I wouldn't call it that exactly. You look like a mountain—take it off quick! You can't possibly be as fat as you appear."

"You look grand to me, Mattie," her mother said, hugging her again, coat and all. "And your friend was thoughtful to lend it to you."

Quite unoffended by the frank criticism

of her appearance, Mrs. Endicott turned to her younger sister.

"You look sleek as a seal, Ann. That New York grooming! There's nothing quite like it, is there, Jan? It seems so perfectly natural and right to find you here, Jan. You've improved. Hasn't she, Mother? Hasn't she, Ann? Who's the man over there? Oh, so that's Tom Hallock. Good-looking—I mean good-looking. Hello, Tom!" She held out her hand. "I know about you. Welcome!"

Everyone laughed, and Tom, who had been feeling a bit de trop, relaxed, quite at home again. Mrs. Endicott's manner was more like Joan's—quick, impulsive and sincere. Hugh was taking his measure, Tom knew, but when he and Mr. Marsh went in to finish their job of putting up the tree, Hugh was close beside him, a friendly hand on his shoulder. The four women went upstairs.

# Chapter Four

❄

*Together Again*

AT LAST the tree was up—a beautiful shapely cedar. The shirt-sleeved men were wrestling with lights when the women came downstairs. Hugh and his father slipped away to the barn and with arms laden crept up the back stairs to Hugh's room, where for some time the two rewrapped and tagged the gifts the old man had bought and those Hugh unearthed from his bags. They carefully deposited their packages on the wide sofa near the tree and were immediately beseiged by inquisitive women.

"Don't you dare touch a thing," Father Marsh warned, "an' don't you even smell, either. Come away from there, Ann. You 'tend to your own knittin'."

For the next few hours there was great excitement, wrapping packages, tying and retying elaborate bows, slipping mysterious gaily wrapped gifts into obscure places, hiding tags and snapping lights on and off to get the effect. Someone started to recite the old favorite:

> " 'Twas the night before Christmas
> And all through the house
> Not a creature was stirring
> Not even a mouse—"

Not one of them could quite complete the long poem, and at times there was just one voice carrying on. However, they all came in strongly at the end:

> "Merry Christmas to all
> And to all a good night!"

There was much clapping of hands and "Bravo!" when the poem was finished, and Martha yawned sleepily and sank into a chair, groaning with fatigue. Her mother slipped over to the old square piano, the others grouped around her. Tom Hallock stood a little apart until Hugh thoughtfully pulled him into the charmed circle. The music was soft.

"Holy night—peaceful night.
All is calm, all is bright,
Round yon Virgin, mother and child,
Holy infant so tender and mild,
Sleep in heavenly pe-ace—
Sleep in heavenly peace."

The old lady's hands dropped from the keys and she raised her happy eyes to those around her.

"Your voices have improved, my dears," she told them, as she had on so many Christmas Eves before. "That was lovely! Now, you children better all scamper off to bed," she urged, "but don't forget to toss down one of your stockings. Father and I will hang them up right here in their old places. Run right along and see you all go straight to sleep or Santa Claus may pass you by.''

How often in the years long past had their mother given that warning, and all but Tom Hallock trooped out and up the long oak stairs. He still stood by the brightly lighted tree. He had no place here—no real place.

''Run get your stocking, Tommy,'' Mother Marsh ordered, ''and one without a hole, too. I declare, you boys must have teeth in your heels.''

''May...may I...hang up my stocking? You mean you really want me to?''

''Of course, son. We'll hang it right here between Janet's and Ann's. When Ann grew up, she insisted on being on the end. She's the baby, you know.''

When Tom brought his sock, Mother Marsh reached up and took his lean face in her two old hands.

''Good night, son. I wish Santa Claus might be very kind to you.''

"Thank you, Mother Marsh. I wish he might. I'm a bit afraid the old boy hasn't time for me, but just being here with you is gift enough. Good night, dear, and sweet dreams!"

"There's one find lad, Lady, an' you know it," Father Marsh stated, and then, aggrieved, "How could our Joan have passed him up for a Charley Austin?"

"There's no accounting for a young girl's fancy, dear, and we'll just have to try to like Joan's husband, whoever he is, though probably it won't make a bit of difference whether we do or not as we're not likely to see much of him. It's getting late, Father—'most 'leven. Bring in that box from the dining-room closet—we'll find plenty of little trinkets there."

The telephone rang and three heads popped out of bedroom doors.

"Who is it?" came from three mouths as Father Marsh took down the receiver.

"Who'd you say? Cannes—France! Mother—Lady—it's Henry! Hurry! All right. Stand right here, dear." He put a sustaining arm around her.

Her voice was faint and tremulous with excitement.

"Speak up, Lady. France is a long ways off." He turned to the telephone. "Hello, boy! Merry Christmas yourself! Here's your mother."

"Oh, it's good to hear you, dear! You did? Yes, filling the stockings, Henry. All but yours and David's. It's all right, dear. We understand. Lots of snow here. Past 'leven. Be a good boy, and our love to Nita. Merry, merry Christmas, Henry! I will. Goodbye!"

She turned shining eyes to her husband. On the next floor, three doors closed softly.

BACK IN THE PARLOR, the old people busied themselves with the stockings, crowding in little gifts, nuts and an orange. The hall clock warned for midnight when a car slid silently along the drive and stopped at the porch. The hall light was still burning, and at the discreet knock Father Marsh flooded the porch with light and flung wide the door. He was prepared for anything now.

"It's Joan, Mother! Why, it's Joan! How did you get here?" He drew her into the hall.

"Flew, darlings! Landed in Syracuse, took a bus to Corinth, hired a taxi to bring me out, and here I am. Got a couple of dollars, Gramp? The fare was ten and I only had eight. Better make it five, darling. He certainly made good time. Here, put this on—whose coat, Gran? Got company?"

"Your Uncle Hugh is here, Joan." The old lady's voice trembled with happiness. "They're all here but your father and Henry, and Henry just now called clear from France—across the Atlantic Ocean!"

"Wh-at! You don't mean Aunt Ann and even Aunt Martha, Gran? 'Way from California!" Joan's eyes were enormous, her mouth a round crimson O of surprise. Then a small secret smile reestablished the perfect Cupid's bow. Her letters had borne fruit.

"I thought tonight was your grand party, my dear," Gran began.

"I ran out on that party, darling. Simply couldn't stick it any longer," Joan explained as she shed her hat and coat and stretched out her hands to the now dying fire. "I'm sick of Aunt Fan's everlasting managing, and lately we've been having a lot of disagreements over Charley Austin. I wish Aunt Fan would marry him herself. I went to Dad, intending to tell him I was making a wide detour, but he was in conference. It seems woodenware is slumping a bit. So I left a note and collected all the loose change I could find and caught the first plane east—and here I am! I won't be forced into marrying a man I don't care a button for just because Aunt Fan and Irma Bessemer think it's good for me."

"Irma Bessemer? Who's she?" her grandfather wanted to know.

"Oh, a charming woman who wants to be my stepmother. Heaven forbid!"

Gramp shook his head and muttered, "Ain't that the limit?"

Gran stammered in surprise, "She—she wants to marry your father? And does he—is he—do you think—"

"I don't know. I hope not. I don't like her—much. For one thing, she's a sort of relative of the Austins. Aunt Fan thinks she's wonderful. To tell the truth, I think Aunt Fan's sick of her job of chaperoning your grandchild. Her brother wants her to go out to Washington to keep house for him. He has no unpredictable young female to keep things stirred up. I wish she would go. I can take care of Dad and myself, too."

She was eyeing the stockings. "Who owns that utilitarian garment, Gran?" indicating the brown-striped woolen sock next to the end.

The old people looked at each other for a moment. "You remember Tom Hallock, Joan? Of course you do," Gran said blandly. "He's spending the holidays with us, and Janet Frost, too."

"T-Tom he-ere!"

Gramp cleared his throat.

"Joan, my dear, you do like Tom! He's such a sweet boy!" her grandmother said softly.

Joan continued to stare at the brown sock. "I know he's sweet, Gran, but he's afraid of me. He's dumb! He thinks I'm selfish and hard and mercenary. He doesn't know that I'm like you, Gran—that I would live on one meal a day in a shack with...with the man I love and be blissfully happy. He thinks I'm modern, worldly, when I'm really the softest, most old-fashioned sentimentalist since the Victorian era!"

"Don't be too sure of that, my girl," her grandfather broke in. "Tom thinks a sight of you, an' we might's well tell you that Mother an' I've decided to let Tom take over this farm—rent it, you understand—in the spring. I bet with his agricultural trainin' he'll make a bigger success of it than a Marsh ever did. Yes, ma'am! The only thing—we would kind of liked to've had a Marsh live here after we pass on, wouldn't we, Mother?"

Joan laughed, a bit tremulously. "You romantic old darling! Trying to bribe your grand-chee-ild?"

"Father, suppose you run away to bed now. I'll just get Joan a bite to eat and we'll be right along. Light up the tree so Joan can see it. Isn't it lovely, dear? And give me one of your stockings—I'll find something to put into it and I'll hang it right here on the end. There—seems like old times. Milk and what else, dear?" as she bustled happily away.

"Just the milk, Gran, and may I have it hot?"

As she sipped the steaming drink, she said little, but her eyes were full of dreams that told the old lady much. At last she rose and stretched her arms high above her lovely head.

"Oh, Gran, it's heaven to be here—tonight! I'm going to sleep right here on this sofa." She laughed. "Maybe I would have to anyway. The house must be full."

"Lovely and full, my dear," Gran said happily. "Tom will be glad to see you."

"I wonder. If I was sure—if I.... Oh
Gran, I love him so, and somehow I feel
sure he loves me, only— Gran, do you
think I dare give him a real gift tomorrow?
Would he accept it, do you think?"

Between them they perfected a plan that
called for much rustling of paper and fit-
ting and pinning here and there, with
plenty of gay Christmas stickers as a final
touch. It took some time, but when Helga
returned from Little Sweden at shortly
before one on Christmas morning, the old
house showed but a single light—the one in
the kitchen.

# Chapter
# Five

*A Special Gift*

CHRISTMASCH!

Noise of someone shaking a furnace
with complete disregard for the feelings of
slumberers roused Tom Hallock from his
usual deep sleep. He sat up bewildered but
after a moment remembered where he
was—the Marsh farm, and it was Christmas morning!

Already his nose told him breakfast was
in the making. Even a dance was powerless
to swerve Helga from her appointed
course. Sausages, fresh bread, coffee—if
that wasn't inducement enough to get people up, he didn't know what was.

He sprang out of bed, wriggled into
dressing gown and slippers, shut his windows, saw the day looked promising,

snatched razor and toothbrush and slipped down the cold hall to the bathroom. Luck was with him: it was empty!

But before he had quite finished shaving he heard slippered footsteps, and someone called loudly, "Merry Christmas in there! But it won't be a Happy New Year, too, if you don't hurry." Then, sotto voce, "It must be Ann. Mat never primps."

"Indeed it isn't Ann." A door had opened down the hall, and Ann's mules flip-flopped nearer.

"Nor, Mat, either, and I'm sure it isn't Jan. I know," Mrs. Endicott, whose feet had made no sound, hissed loudly. "It's that handsome Tom Hallock!"

Tom opened the door, smiling broadly.

"I'm sorry I kept you waiting, but if you will lie abed mornings—Merry Christmas!"

Ann ducked into the bathroom while Hugh's back was turned and slid the bolt. Martha pounded on the door.

"Let me in, too." The door was cautiously opened and Martha slipped in. Hugh sighed resignedly.

"That's always the way in this house—girls first." He sat down on the floor beside the door and pulled his robe more snugly around his lean body. "By Jove! I'll be next or know the reason why!"

Tom went into his own room. What a swell bunch they were! Half an hour later he trooped down to breakfast with the others.

The old people seemed even more excited than on the night before and kept exchanging cautioning glances. Once a smothered sneeze came from the closed parlor where the tree stood ready to yield up its mysteries.

"Santa Claus!" cried Mattie, her head cocked, listening.

"That was no male sneeze, Mat," Hugh scoffed, and caught a look of dismay on his mother's face. "Unless," he added quickly, "the old gentleman's voice is changing or he's sent a proxy, as so often happens in these modern days."

"Probably Helga," Ann contributed, reaching for another hot roll, and wondered at the relieved glance her mother and father exchanged.

Something was going on that they didn't know about. Her mother and father were making a very light breakfast and seemed childishly eager to see their gifts.

At last Mother Marsh could stand it no longer. Was ever a breakfast more leisurely?

"Won't you ever finish?" she cried. "It's Christmas! Haven't any of you a bit of curiosity? I'm sure Santa Claus has been wonderful to us all. Come on, Father. Let us go." She caught his hand and led the way down the hall.

There were most intriguing bulges in each of the eight stockings—eight? *Helga's no doubt,* Tom said to himself, *although she never wore that stocking, I'll bet a dollar,* eyeing the sheer gray silk length.

Ann stared for a moment, and her father unfastened her brown stocking and handed it to her. Tom was amused as she squealed like a small girl at the funny doll pin-cushion on top.

"You're next, Tom." Mother Marsh gave him a little shove, making mysterious silent but urgent motions for the others to follow her from the room. Dutifully, they obeyed.

Tom gazed fascinated at the big, ir-regular bundle, conical in shape and tied with a huge red bow. It was attached to the toe of his sock by more red ribbon and on the card—no, it couldn't be—"From Joan."

The others, bright eyed and eager, were questioning Mother Marsh just outside the door, but she shushed them with the whis-pered, "All in good time—just a special Christmas gift for Tom."

Impatient at the continued silence in the parlor, Father Marsh poked his head in at the door. What ailed the boy? Gran tugged at his arm, but the old man cried excitedly, "Gosh, Tom! You're slower'n molasses in January. Show some speed!"

Mystified and somewhat dazed, Tom

pulled the bow, and a flushed and shyly smiling face looked up at him. The eyes, however, were not smiling. Wide and a bit afraid, they gazed at the astonished young man, and Gran's hand crept into her husband's as she gently but firmly closed the door.

"Joan—darling!" Tom was on his knees beside her.

"Do—do you like your Christmas gift?" Then with his arms close around her, "Oh, Tommy! You big, wonderful dumbbell! Why didn't you tell me last summer? Think of all these months we've wasted!"

IT WAS SOME TIME LATER that they awoke to the fact that they were quite alone and that stockings still hung, bulging with secrets, from the chimney shelf. Sounds of laughter and chatter came from beyond the door, and Joan sprang to her feet.

"What pigs we are, Tom! Gran, Gramp—all of you! Come on back! We've landed!"

"So's your old man!" chortled her

grandfather with surprising promptness. "Dave landed about fifteen minutes ago. Due here in an hour. Said he was sorry to be late. What I'd like to know is, was it just happenchance your all comin' home like this, or was it planned?"

Nobody answered—they didn't have a chance, for Joan cried, "Oh, grand! You'll love Dad, Tom. He's a peach when you get him away from business—and Aunt Fan. Let's hang up a stocking for him and I'll. . . I'll give him a son."

"What he needs is a wife," murmured David's mother to her husband. "I wish. . . ." And her eyes rested on Janet's smiling face as she helped the others collect things for David's stocking.

"No, Mother. Better keep hands off there. He didn't appreciate her once an' 'tain't likely he will now. Matchmakin' ain't much in our line, I guess," cautioned the old man.

"No-o? Well, maybe not." But her eyes smiled and she gave him a gentle shove.

IT WAS an aggrieved David Marsh who sprang up the steps an hour later. He kissed his mother, sisters and, quite matter-of-factly, Janet Frost. (She felt sure he hadn't even seen her.) He shook hands with his father and brother, scolded the unrepentant Joan and eyed with grim suspicion the young man Joan presented to him as his Christmas gift from her.

He made it plain he neither wanted nor needed a son at this particular time, and Joan was far too young to know her own mind.

His sisters jeered at him and followed their mother upstairs. They were all going to church, and there was work to be done first. Hugh and his father went out to the barn.

"Don't be selfish, David," Janet Frost whispered, noting his black looks. "Ellen wasn't as old as Joan when you married her. Joan's a lucky girl, for Tom Hallock is a man in a million."

"But they tell me they want to live

here—on this farm! Joan will die of loneliness," countered David.

"Fiddlesticks! Those two will never be lonely while they have each other. As for this farm, look at your mother and father. Look at them. Are they lonely? I ask you. A happier, more contented pair I have never known.

"Even when their five children failed continually, mind you, to keep their holiday tryst at the old home, they weren't beaten. Like an army with banners they marched on down the years, smiling above the hurts and reaching out gracious hands to draw lone strays into their charmed circle.

"No, David, don't pity Joan; she is like your mother, a sweet soul. Pity yourself, rather, that you have let woodenware dull your finer perceptions, blind you to the beauties, the worthwhile things, of life.

"I have known you all for a long time, David, but lately I had begun to dislike you Marsh children for a lot of smug, selfish worldlings. Not one of you is worthy of your mother and father.

"I have hopes of Joan. Perhaps she will redeem the family. She is your one excuse for living, David—the lot of you. The sole reward of your parents' years of pain and sacrifice."

"Whew!" gasped David Marsh, mopping his forehead, undecided whether to be angry or merely amused. "Straight from the shoulder as always, Jan. But at that you're right. Right on several counts. Joan does love the old place. Queer, too—now that you speak of it, I can see that she is like Mother. I don't think I ever noticed it before." But just the same, he had no intention of losing Joan for a while yet.

He looked into the clear, serene brown eyes of the woman beside him and thought how wholesome she was. How sweetly comfortable!

Let's see, he had been rather badly smitten on Janet Frost during their high-school days. He wondered just why they had drifted apart. Keen mind, Janet had, and wonderfully kind to the old folks.

He remembered suddenly how he and Janet, back in the old days, had planned long voyages—to South America, the Orient, Egypt and the South Seas. Well, why not—someday? Did she really dislike him so much, or was it possible to rekindle that old feeling? It might be worth trying. He was going to be terribly lonely when Joan left him, as she certainly would eventually.

He had a swift picture of Janet Frost in the library at home. In the drawing room receiving guests with her charming dignity. Presiding at his table. He looked at her again and she smiled.

"Not angry at me, David?"

"Angry? Of course not, Jan. Didn't we always bare our hearts and minds to each other?"

"No one answered Father Marsh's question, David. Who was it planned this grand surprise? Your mother looks years younger."

David shook his head. "Just as I was leaving my office I received a wire from Hugh saying they were all coming home for the holidays. When I reached home, Joan had already gone. If I had known...." He was plainly distressed. David never was one to follow. He led.

"It doesn't matter," Janet murmured, "just so long as you are all here."

# Chapter Six

❄

*Just like Old Times*

THERE WERE ARGUMENTS and much good-
natured raillery before the Marsh family
and their guests were packed into the two
cars and on their way to the little church in
Wellsburg.

Ann refused to let Martha go to the
village looking like a moth-eaten fullback.
Martha protested that only one tiny spot
showed any signs of moths and Ann
shouldn't be so snooty. No one would
notice what she had on—people never did.

At last Joan, who was taller than either
of her aunts, settled the argument by don-
ning the coat in question, holding it
wrapped tightly around her hips and
pirouetting before them.

"See!" she laughed, as Gran nodded in

approval. "You wear mine, Aunt Mat. You needn't fasten it. Just leave this woolen scarf loose—so. We'll be riding." She helped her faintly protesting aunt into the smart Persian lamb that had been her father's last birthday gift to her, and stepped back.

"You should wear black, Aunt Mat. It does wonderful things for you. Slims you down and makes your complexion and eyes simply thrilling!"

"You're a sweet child, Joan," Aunt Mat declared, tucking a stray lock of hair beneath her small black hat. "But I wouldn't wear it if Ann, my own sister, weren't ashamed of me in that raccoon."

Ann dabbed a bit of powder on her sister's nose before she answered. "Untidy and careless as you are, Martha, my own, you're a grand girl, and I love you!"

"That's nice." Martha smiled happily. "We're an awfully nice-looking family when we're dressed up, aren't we?"

"You bet we are!" Hugh agreed from the doorway. "But we're never on time. If you girls are going to church this morning, let's get started.''

They made quite a stir in the little church as they marched down the aisle to the pews the Marshes had occupied for nearly half a century. The old people entered first and Hugh and his sisters followed. Joan and her father, with Janet Frost and Tom Hallock, sat in front. Heads turned. There were smiles and nods. Gran's eyes held a glory that never was on land or sea.

"Unto you a child is born; unto you a son is given...."

Joan's hand slipped into her father's and his closed tightly over it. The little church smelled of spruce and cedar. Red candles in tall silver candelabra flanked the pulpit, their flames flickering constantly. Old Dr. Lester beamed upon his congregation, his face ruddy, his eyes benign.

"And there were in the same country shepherds abiding in the field...."

Joan stole a glance at her father. She wondered if he was finding all this as wonderful and satisfying as she did. A choir of sweet but untrained voices was singing the anthem: "...a son is given—a son is given...."

She squeezed her father's fingers and he looked down at her—and smiled. She leaned a little forward the better to see Tom. He, too, turned his head and smiled. Her heart felt bursting with happiness.

The sermon was not long; woven through with precious familiar words:

"Fear not; for behold, I bring you good tidings of great joy...."

Joan knew she was never to forget this service. They were standing for the final hymn.

"O Little Town of Bethlehem,
    How still we see thee lie
    Above thy deep and dreamless sleep
    The silent stars go by;
    Yet in thy dark streets shineth
    The everlasting light;

The hopes and fears of all the years
Are met in thee tonight.''

From behind her came the slightly
tremulous voice of Gran and the still lusty
one of Gramp. They were all singing. Uncle Hugh's deep voice could be heard
above all the rest. Dad never sang at home,
but here he was singing and enjoying it.

"O holy Child of Bethlehem!
Descend on us, we pray;
Cast out our sin, and enter in;
Be born in us today.
We hear the Christmas angels
The great glad tidings tell;
O come to us, abide with us,
Our Lord Emmanuel!''

The benediction: "Now to the Father,
Son and Holy Ghost...."
Down from the pulpit came Dr. Lester.
Friends, old schoolmates surrounded the
Marshes, and Joan and Tom Hallock
slipped away.

"Let's walk part of the way, Tom," Joan suggested happily. "I know that crowd. They're good for half an hour at least. Isn't it all grand, Tommy?"

"I'm afraid your father isn't very happy about us, darling," the young man said dubiously. "I can't altogether blame him."

"Oh, he'll come around," Joan assured him. "This has been a grand Christmas, Tommy. I think the happiest I have ever had—since I've been grown up."

"It's been wonderful! You're a fine family, Joan—from the old gentleman down. I wonder why they all decided to come home, though. Mr. and Mrs. Marsh didn't expect them. That's why they invited Miss Frost and me."

Joan laughed softly. "You'd be surprised if I told you, darling, and I think I'm not going to—at least not yet."

Raucous horns blared behind them. The first car passed, honking derisively. The second stopped.

"Get in, you two." It was Ann who

opened the door. "You're still three miles from home and the rest of us are hungry, even if you aren't. Are you by any chance laboring under the delusion it's summer?"

"Why, it's not a bit cold, Aunt Ann," protested Joan. "One couldn't be cold in this coat."

"That coat!" jeered Ann. "And to think Mat will have to wear it home—across the continent! One thing, though, she's going back by train and can have a section to herself." But her twinkling eyes belied her disgusted tone. It was only that her own fashionable mink coat made her dissatisfied with anything less for her sister.

"Oh, who cares?" Martha sang from the front seat. "But I do feel smooth in your coat, Joan. I almost wish I had a chance to wear furs occasionaly. They're certainly flattering to one's figure." She laughed again and wrinkled her nose at her sister. "After all, there's nothing like a good old New York State Christmas, is there?"

"Oh, it isn't the place so much as it is the

people," Ann elaborated. "Wherever home happened to be—there the Marshes could keep Christmas, you know."

"I hope that turkey is as big as Pop said it was," Hugh muttered from behind the wheel.

Joan looked at Tom. Clothes! Food! What did such things matter on a day like this?

THEY WERE SEATED around the table in the long dining room. Nine of them. A great bowl of holly was on the big sideboard and holly and lighted red candles on the table. Silence and bowed heads when Gramp rose in his place for grace.

"For Thy many blessings, we thank Thee, our Heavenly Father. For love an' health, for food an' shelter, we thank Thee. For Thy son whose birthday we celebrate, we thank Thee, and as parent to parent, dear God—Thou knowest how thankful we are that our children are home again. That they are still loyal to the old home. Mother an' I thank Thee. Amen."

There was a long moment of complete silence. Three pairs of eyes—slightly misty—focused on Joan, who shook her head, finger on lips.

"Want me to carve, Father?" David asked, although he knew he wouldn't be allowed.

"No. No. I'll do the carving, Dave. I'm still the champeen carver in Wakeeta County. Eh, Lady?"

Mother Marsh nodded. David didn't fool her a bit. David had always disliked any display of emotion.

"Right nice havin' a big family again, ain't it, Mother?" Gramp went on, skillfully whetting the carving knife that had been carefully sharpened against this occasion.

"Don't forget, Pop. The thigh and drumstick and plenty of stuffing for me," Hugh reminded his father. "Save the white meat for the girls."

Tom found it hard to reconcile this very homely, still boyishly droll man with the distinguished Hugh Marsh, famous corporation lawyer. Joan caught his puzzled glance and giggled.

"Hunger knows no class distinction, Tommy," she murmured. "Uncle Hugh adores turkey."

"You bet I do, my child," her uncle admitted.

"What keen ears you have!" Joan was slightly abashed. After all, Uncle Hugh was...well, Hugh Marsh!

"The better to hear testimony with, my dear," he retorted, smiling at her. "So you think you want to be a farmer's wife, do you?" he asked quizzically.

Joan gasped and looked across the table at her father, who was eating celery and talking to Janet Frost.

"So she says." David Marsh swallowed his mouthful and reached for his water glass.

Janet whispered, "Bravo!" and he caught her hand beneath the table.

"And what Joan wants, she usually gets," David Marsh went on.

"Thank you, sir." Tom Hallock stood

up. David Marsh stood up. They shook hands across the table. "I'll see you never have cause to regret your decision, sir."

"Now that that's settled and out of the way, suppose you continue, er, begin carving, Pop," Hugh said whimsically. "I haven't received that thigh and drumstick with lots of stuffing yet."

Father Marsh glanced down the long table and continued the deliberate, tantalizing honing. A long exasperated sigh went up. The candles flickered. Gran and Gramp exchanged mirthful glances. This was the regular procedure at Christmas dinners. Nothing was changed. The family knew what to expect and sat back with exaggerated resignation.

"'Member that first Christmas, Mother, an' how we had a cute little tree an' hung a catnip ball onto it for the cat an' a box of newfangled dog biscuits for old...Rex, 'twas, wasn't it? 'Member how we drove over to Wellsburg to church an' what a lovely mornin' it was? Seems like I'll never forget that first Christmas—"

"No-o," groaned Hugh and Martha in unison, leaning against each other in complete and utter exhaustion, "nor will we!"

For a moment the old man looked nonplussed, shocked at the interruption; then his eyes twinkled as he glance down the length of the table again. Mother was smiling. Swiftly he set to work. There was a great deal of laughter and well-meaning but entirely ignored advice. Each plate was piled high and passed.

The old man settled into his chair and picked up his knife and fork. Once again his glance went down the length of the table, paused at each happy, absorbed face and then went on to the next.

Thank God that his children were still loyal to the old traditions, old customs, and that their hearts and footsteps turned homeward at Christmastime!